For Ethan Long, one great quarterback! —T. F.

For Travis Foster. Thank you for bringing me back to life. —E. L.

Manufactured in China.

Library of Congress Cataloging-in-Publication Data:

Names: Foster, Travis, author, illustrator. | Long, Ethan, author,
illustrator.
Title: Give me back my book! / Travis Foster and Ethan Long.
Description: San Francisco, California : Chronicle Books, [2017] |
Summary: Two friends, Redd and Bloo, argue over the possession of one
special book with a green cover, hard cover, a nice spine, and pages that
turn from right to left—but unite when Bookworm walks off with it.
Identifiers: LCCN 2016033214 | ISBN 9781452160405 (alk. paper)
Subjects: LCSH: Books and reading—Juvenile fiction. |
Possessiveness—Juvenile fiction. | Friendship—Juvenile fiction. | CYAC:
Books and reading—Fiction. | Friendship—Fiction.
Classification: LCC PZ7.1.F677 Gi 2017 | DDC [E]—dc23 LC record
available at https://lccn.loc.gov/2016033214

Design by Travis Foster and Ethan Long.
Photographs by Michael David Foster.
The three characters in this book were rendered digitally and
separately by Mr. Foster (Redd and Bookworm) and Mr. Long (Bloo).
Mr. Long digitally assembled all of the images into each illustration.

10 9 8 7 6 5 4 3 2 1

Chronicle Books LLC
680 Second Street
San Francisco, California 94107

Chronicle Books—we see things differently.
Become part of our community at www.chroniclekids.com.

Give Me Back MY Book!

Travis Foster and Ethan Long

chronicle books·san francisco

There are **letters** on each page and they are gathered together to form **words** that have meaning when you read them!

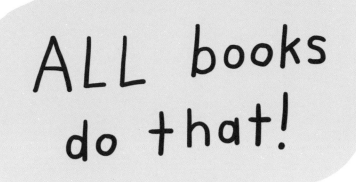

Oh yes, but my book has a table of contents, funny little things called chapters, and every now and again there is something called an illustration.

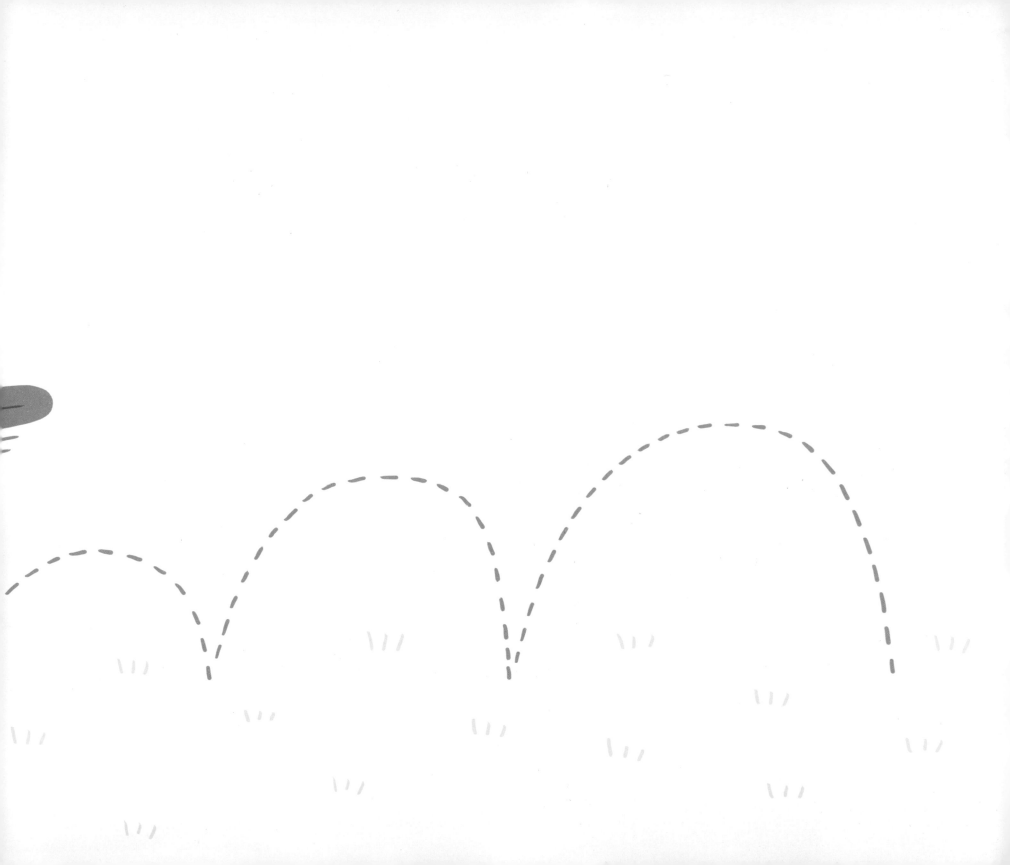

This will make the perfect bait!
Yes! The cover, spine, and pages will be hard to resist.
GLOO

The illustrations
will make her
eyes explode!
GLOO
PINK
RED
PURPLE

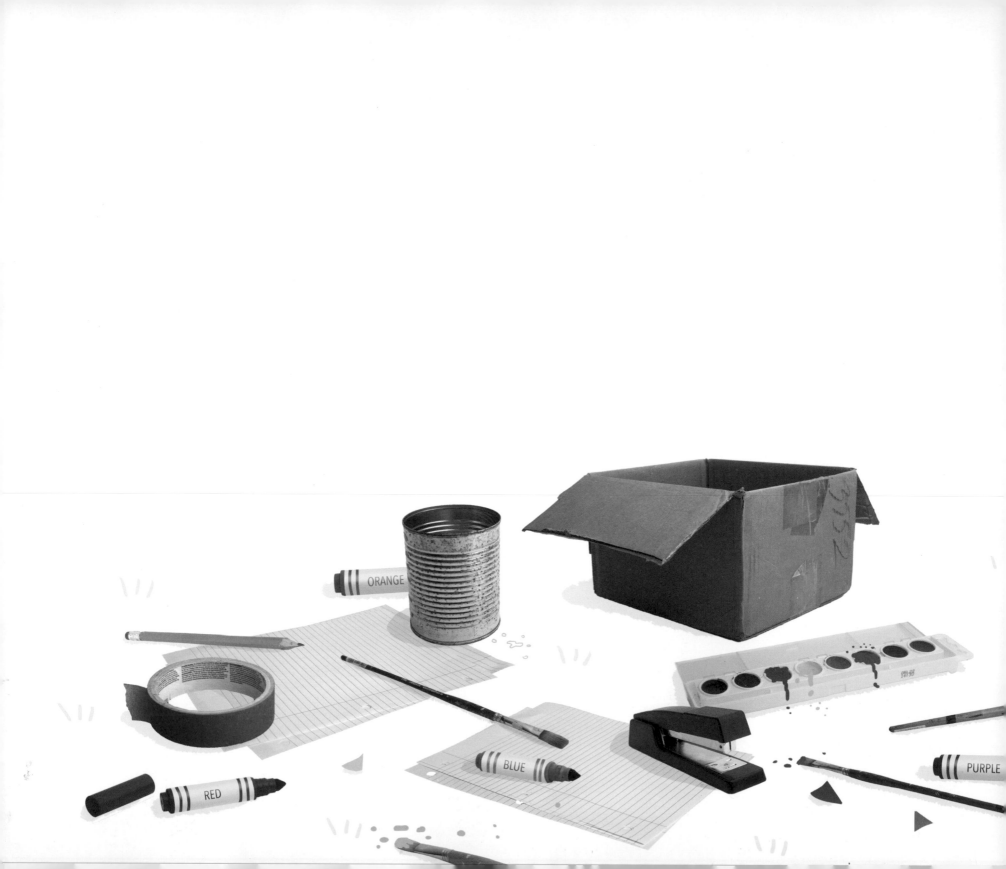

HA!

The End